SCOUT
and ACE

Kissing Frogs

Written by Rose Impey
Illustrated by Ant Parker

Once upon a time, our heroes,

SCOUT and **ACE**

set out on a trip

into outer, outer-space.

Sucked through a worm-hole...

to a strange, new place,

lost in a galaxy called Fairy Tale Space.

"Let's go left and check it out," says Scout.

When Scout and Ace land on the planet Frogonia they find a glass case.

Inside is a sleeping frog-princess.

"Let's wake her up," says Ace.
"I bet she can tell us about this place."

Ace taps hard on the glass.

But the frog-princess doesn't wake.

Even when Ace gives the case
a good shake,

she still doesn't wake.

Just then seven little Men from Mars come racing towards them.

"Quick, let's get out," shouts Scout.

Scout and Ace race off.

They race straight into a trap.

The little men tell Scout and Ace,
"A wizard called Quell put a
spell on the princess."

Ace tells Scout, "If we want to get out of this place, one of us will have to kiss that frog."

Ace groans. He gives the frog a light peck on the cheek but the frog doesn't even peek.

The frog is so slimy, the next kiss almost misses.

Ace wishes it had.

In the end Ace gives the frog
a great, big, fat, smacking kiss
that sounds like this:

Then, faster than it takes to tell, the kiss breaks the spell. The princess wakes and all is well.

Well, almost.

The princess begs Scout and
Ace to stay . . .

. . . but Ace can't wait to get away.

Scout says, "We may come
back another day."

But Ace says, "No way!"

"That was close," says Ace. "Hey, Captain, what do you call a girl with a frog on her head? Lily! Boom! Boom!"

"Oh dear," groans Scout.
"Time to get out of here."

Fire the engines...

and lower the dome.

Once more our heroes...

are heading for home.

Enjoy all these stories about

SCOUT and ACE

and their adventures in Space

Scout and Ace: Kippers for Supper
1 84362 172 X

Scout and Ace: Flying in a Frying Pan
1 84362 171 1

Scout and Ace: Stuck on Planet Gloo
1 84362 173 8

Scout and Ace: Kissing Frogs
1 84362 176 2

Scout and Ace: Talking Tables
1 84362 174 6

Scout and Ace: A Cat, a Rat and a Bat
1 84362 175 4

Scout and Ace: Three Heads to Feed
1 84362 177 0

Scout and Ace: The Scary Bear
1 84362 178 9

All priced at £4.99 each.

Colour Crunchies are available from all good bookshops, or can be ordered direct from the publisher
Orchard Books, PO BOX 29, Douglas MM99 1BQ.
Credit card orders please telephone 01624 836000 or fax 01624 837033
or email: bookshop@enterprise.net for details.

To order please quote title, author and ISBN and your full name and address. Cheques and postal
orders should be made payable to 'Bookpost plc'. Postage and packing is FREE within the UK –
overseas customers should add £1.00 per book. Prices and availability are subject to change.

ORCHARD BOOKS, 96 Leonard Street, London EC2A 4XD.
Orchard Books Australia, 32/45-51 Huntley Street, Alexandria, NSW 2015.
This edition first published in Great Britain in hardback in 2004. First paperback publication 2005.
Text © Rose Impey 2004. Illustrations © Ant Parker 2004. The rights of Rose Impey to be identified as
the author and Ant Parker to be identified as the illustrator have been asserted by them in accordance with the
Copyright, Designs and Patents Act, 1988. A CIP catalogue record for this book is available from the British Library.
ISBN 1 84362 176 2   10 9 8 7 6 5 4 3 2
Printed in China